Music in the Garden of Evil
Book II

Music and the Star of David

Inner Sound Books
Savannah, Georgia

Music and the Star of David

ISBN 978-0-9801614-1-0

Dedication

For my mother, Betty Lee, for my father, H. David Lee, for my sister, Lorriana, for my Grandparents, and for the Lee and Johnson Family. I come from the deep roots of a proud tree planted by living waters.

CHAPTER 1

SHE WAS PROBABLY VERY beautiful as a child. Her angelic voice must have filled this church with so much joy. But we may never know, because now she is deathly ill. She has been poisoned by a demon shadow who was after her secret. She was shown no mercy. She needs your help. She is the Ancient Spirit of the Music Ministry.

I am Otto, Chief Music Teacher of the Secrets of Music. I want to welcome you to *Music and the Star of David*. I promise that the things I share with you in this book will open your mind and change your life. This story is not a source of entertainment. This is the story of God's purpose and plan for music. You are about to read an ancient scroll that has finally been unearthed after centuries of secrecy. Many men have lost their lives protecting this secret scroll; all the while knowing that one day many music minities would desperately need musical direction. And now is that time. Now we are entering the END OF AGE!

So take this story and share it with others who want to know musical praise from the highest levels. You must promise to share this word, or I beg you, please do not read any further. This scroll is too powerful to be left in idle hands. Perhaps I have told you too much. But you will be changed by the reading this revelation, because this revelation comes from God!

The writers of time once wrote that 'ignorance is bliss'. So verily I say unto you, once you read this sacred scroll of music, there will be no returning back to a state of musical ignorance. Yet every word you read is breaking Satan's musical strongholds over you, and he knows it. He wants you to stop reading. But keep reading and keep breaking the strongholds!

Let me now tell you the story of my travels to the Village of Misguided Music.

CHAPTER 2

ONCE A MONTH I took the Disciples of Christian Music on a mission trip. We traveled throughout the known world spreading the Gospel of Jesus Christ, teaching the principles of Christian music, and rescuing people from the musical strongholds of Satan. During our travels many souls were saved and many songs were delivered. But we were not always welcomed with opened arms. On this mission trip, we came across a village of people that believed their music could do no wrong.

The head musician of the village approached me in a tone of arrogance and said, "Old-man Otto, I have heard of you. You and your disciples of misfits think that you hold some secret of music. You think you can tell the world how to make music and how to listen to it. Who are you to judge us?"

I peacefully replied, "I am no judge, but you will be judged by a law that has been in existence since God created the earth. You will be judged by a law that was written before the written word, God's Law of Sound."

"You are a fool. I create the music that I play. My musical mind is so vast that I imagine great sounds, and the sounds flow through me!" he shouted.

Keeping my peace, I replied, "Well, you may be imagining from a heart that is evil. So from whose imagination should I trust? Should I trust music that is not based on principle? To what standards of measure do you weigh your music against? Jesus told us to be careful what we listen to; for the same standard of measure will be used against you (Mark 4:24). You did not get your musical laws from the Bible, because the Divine Laws of Sounds are not stated as such." This angered many of the village musicians.

"Our music could never be evil. Why do you speak of such heresy in our village? The church cannot make evil music! Otto, you are a blasphemer and a heretic. People of the village, do not listen to this fool!" shouted the head musician in an angry tone. His eyes capsized in a sea of red, tones of hate filled his head. His emotions had overtaken his reason. Pride was his deadly sin.

But with grace, I replied, "You doubt me, and I like that! You should doubt me. Oh my, what proof do I have? Ah yes, here it is!" I pulled out my Bible and opened to the book of Genesis. "Here it is! I am so terribly sorry for my delay, but this scripture will be worth it. The word of God rings much louder than my own. Little boy, yes you in the corner; be a good boy and read this scripture aloud for all of the people to hear."

So the boy slowly walked towards me and took hold of the Bible. Then, in a frightened little voice, the boy read:

"... *the imagination of man's heart is evil from his youth,* Genesis 8:21. Sir Otto, am I evil?" the little boy asked so innocently.

"No, you are not evil. You are a good boy. Now run along." The Disciples of Christian Music began to laugh; they knew I used a child to strengthen my argument. "Does your music have boundaries, or is it free to roam like a wild beast? My Bible tells me that people '*speak evil of those things which they know not: but what they know naturally, as but beast, in those things they corrupt themselves*' (Jude 1:10). Does your Bible say that?"

With a grit of his teeth, the head musician of the village answered, "My Bible does says that, but---"

I interrupted in a questioning tone. "So, you do not understand the Principles of Christian Music, but you speak evil against it. Yet, you also praise the music that comes from your evil imagination. Well, something about that does not sound right. My fellow Christian, does the music that you are putting into your soul reflect what you want to come out? Remember: evil begets evil, pain begets pain, but love begets love."

His head fell low, and with humility he replied, "You are right, Otto. I apologize for my harsh tone. Please teach us the Principles of Christian Music. Our music is without principle and without a standard of measure."

"Of course I will teach you. That is my mission as a Disciple of Christian Music. The first thing you must know is God's purpose for music:

TO GLORIFY GOD AND TO EDIFY MAN

Next, you must know the three main principles of Christian Music:

Be Ye Led By the Spirit
Be Ye Rooted in Christ
Be Ye Wise in Musical Knowledge

"Now we will learn the meanings of the sound-fruit and all about Music in the Garden of Good and Evil. Spread these truths throughout your village so the people will learn musical discernment. Teach the parents so they will know how to speak to their children about music. Spread these truths so that pastors can be as good shepherds guarding the ears of their flock. If the eyes are the windows to the soul, then the ears are the back door. I say unto you; a lack of knowledge is no excuse in the Body of Christ. For the Bible says,

'With all thy getting, get (an) understanding' (Proverbs 4:7). So understand this well, and your music can be made whole.

"The Bible tells us about Satan's music and his fall from Heaven (*Your pomp and the music of your harps have brought you down to Sheol.* Isaiah 14:11). Your music can cause you to miss out on God's many blessings. Satan's music brought him down to Sheol; which is another name for Hades, Hell, and the place of the dead. The Bible says that the music of Satan brought out his evil and caused him to be thrown into the place of the dead. The devil is still learning his lesson. But you are a wise and good man in search of the truth. So allow me to lead you into the green pasture of Truth and away from a burning fate.

"Your village would not want a doctor lacking in medical knowledge to operate on a sick child, would it? But as for the one who blindly ministers to your soul in the language of music, you do not speak against. For if you were fluent in this language, you would know that an unskilled musician could be spreading lies that even he believes!

"The Bible teaches us about the meaning of music. '*Yet even lifeless things, either flute or harp, in producing a sound, if they do not produce a distinction in the tones, how will it be known what is played on the flute or on the harp? For if the bugle produces an indistinct sound, who will prepare himself for battle? There* are, perhaps, a great many languages in the world, and no kind is without meaning.' (I Corinthians 14:7-8,10 NASB)

"I Thessalonians 4:16 says, '*For the Lord Himself will descend from Heaven with a shout, with the voice of the archangel and with the sound of the trumpet, and the dead in Christ will rise first.*' Now it is time to raise the dead. Now is the time to raise those dead churches and dead ministries out of the valley of dry bones! Now is the time to praise with purpose and worship with principle! So let us raise our praise to the highest level and be heard with a mighty shout!" And all of the people shouted praises unto the Lord. Glory be to God!

Now this is how every mission trip was for the Disciples of Christian Music. This is the mission that the Lord has given me, and I have been secretly passing it on to you with every word that you have been reading. I will not always be here to tell this story. So you must learn these principles and pass them on to everyone with a heart of worship. Pass this knowledge to those worshippers in the same manner it was passed to you. Teach them this parable. But ask yourself; do you have the courage to share these truths?

CHAPTER 3

I SEE THAT YOU have chosen the brave path by your continued reading; you have much courage. You remind me of the courage I saw in the eyes of the Disciples of Christian Music. That same courage was in the eyes of my supporters at the steps of the church in the Kingdom of Mir. I remember that day well.

The crowd of supporters drew near. The entire kingdom knew the works of the Disciples of Christian Music. I addressed the people, stating, "Three points I make for you today: **The biggest book in the Bible, Psalms, is dedicated to music!!! The Longest chapter in the Bible, Psalm 119:1-176, is dedicated to music!!! The center of the Bible, Psalm 118, is dedicated to music!!!** And you dare not take music with the utmost seriousness?

"The Bible says that man is inherently a sinner. If your music is rooted in your own desires, would not your music be that of a sinner. If the nature of man is sin, then the nature of your musical desire is sin. So we, as Christians, need musical deliverance to have the assurance that our music is guided by holy principles.

But we do not have to look far for the wisdom of God. His plan for musical wisdom and guidance can be seen throughout the Bible:

Be Led by the Spirit (Galatians 5:18)
Be Rooted in Christ (Ephesians 3:17)
Study to Show Thyself Approved (II Timothy 2:15)

"If you are the type of person that says, 'I do not worry about such things, I just play music', then I will ask you this. If you led your life the same way you led your music, would you be pleasing God or pleasing yourself? If you led your life the same way you played your music, would you be in Heaven or Hell after your life is over? Let us look from a higher view. God is a God of purpose, order, and design. It is easy to make music. And yes, it is even easier to play someone else's music. But it is holy to understand and create music according to God's Purpose.

"And what is God's purpose for music: TO GLO-RIFY GOD AND TO EDIFY MAN (I Corinthians 10:31 & 14:26). Music is a gift from God that is given to us with a sign on the box saying 'SOME AS-SEMBLY REQUIRED'. You must understand how music is put together. You must put your music to-gether with the blueprint of purpose and the tool-belt of principle. As a listener of music, you must know the fruits of sound from which your ears feast upon.

My Bible says in Proverbs 1:7 that the '*Fear of the Lord is the beginning of knowledge*'. And if you fear the Lord, should you not also fear His Laws of Sound and His Principles of Music? Do not conform to the music of this world, but let your music be transformed by the renewal of your mind!"

The crowd cheered for the wisdom that had been shared. But suddenly the royal guards were seen pushing their way through the crowd. I stood still with no fear as the guards approached me.

"We have orders from the king to arrest you, Otto! Come with us at once. You will go to the bottom of the jail for your heresy," laughed the head guard.

The crowd became angry so I calmed them; there was no need for the peaceful listeners to get hurt. I told my disciples to have no fear. Then I gave my most trusted student, Bashiri, instructions to travel to the Garden of Good and Evil in order to seek guidance from Percy. And the guards took me away to the royal dungeon with great haste.

CHAPTER 4

UPON REACHING THE GATES of the garden, Bashiri began to feel the warmth of the presence of God. He entered the garden after being questioned by the gatekeeper. Once inside of the garden, Bashiri heard peaceful sounds like the crystal tingling of wind chimes. The summer breeze traveled gently between the leaves of sound-fruit trees. And there was Percy on bended knee digging and pruning around the first tree of three.

"You know, you really have to dig deeply into this brown ground if you really want the best sound. Well, hello my friend. Welcome to the Garden of Good and Evil. My name is Percy, and I am the gardener. It is from this garden that all sounds are birthed," said Percy in a friendly tone.

A smile grew over Bashiri's face, "Wonderful, my name is Bashiri. This garden is so beautiful that I can hardly believe my eyes and ears. Oh my, is that a sound-tree bearing actual sound-fruit? I am so happy to finally see this garden with my own eyes. But before I get lost in the wonders of the garden, I must fulfill my mission and deliver to you this message from Otto." It was then that Bashiri told Percy about the jailing of Otto by King Clef's guards. He also told Percy about a strange new sound that had been coming from the castle top.

"Percy, I am told you are wise and know all of the secrets of music. I would like to know about God's Law of Sound. I have learned the Principles of Music, the Meanings of the Sounds, The Nature of Man and Music, the Parables, and the Doctrine of Sound Combination. But I would like very much to know about God's Laws of Sound."

"My friend, I see why Otto sent you. You are the curious one. Otto told me about you. Come, let us sit and talk. You must prepare your heart for God's Law of Sound."

Percy took Bashiri deep into the garden until they reached a heavily wooded area. "If you want to know the Law of Sound, you must enter the cave found in the heart of the garden.

"Once you have reached the depths of the cave, look for a book with the word, SELAH, engraved on the cover. Now, are you sure that you are ready for this knowledge? Many men have died trying to get these secrets, and those who survived spent years trying to forget it. Once you open that book there is no turning back. Your mind must be ready!"

Bashiri did not show the slightest bit of hesitation.

"I am ready to learn God's Law of Sound. It is my duty as a Christian musician to know this law."

Percy smiled and said, "Very well, my brother. But before you enter the cave, I want to share with you two stories about the powerful effects of music on the family. Now, first things first. Let us pray to the Lord for wisdom and understanding." After the prayer, Percy began to share new stories that had never crossed my ears. The stories were known as *The Spirit of Depression* and *The Song of a Warrior.*

The Spirit of Depression

"I once knew a man that was plagued with the spirit of depression. But there was a reason for his depression. This man listened to minor sound-fruit all day; his spirit fed upon it. The more he ate; the more he craved. The more he craved; the more he ate. His spirit was soon overtaken by his emotions. The sadness locked within the minor sound-fruit had been as wood to the fire of his depression. Soon the misery of the fruit became his friend. The fire grew out of his control! His misery enjoyed the company of the minor sound-fruit. Misery enjoys company.

"This man's family began to hear the sound of his voice changing key. His life became such a sad song that his family could no longer be in tune with him. His song was once loving and kind. But the sound of his voice had since grown cold, his eyes turned a hazy shade of dead man's gray, and his sound-fruit turned a depressed shade of gloom. A rotten sound-fruit became his stormy soul; his life had taken on the spirit of depression.

"Then one day his innocent little daughter held his hand and let out a tear, saying, 'Daddy, don't you love me anymore?' His head sank fast into his hands. His heart hit the floor. The father became slain with the spirit of shame. He thought, 'What sad song have I sung to my little girl? She is hearing the sad sound of my voice, and my song is becoming her song. I must change keys! The flavor of my sound-fruit has been minor, but from now on I will release the sweet, orange nectar of the major sound-fruit.'

"So the father released major sound-fruit all over the room as he sang to his daughter, 'Daddy loves you, Daddy loves you!' The room suddenly filled with a warm glow of orange and blue. His daughter's eyes filled with joy, and she smiled from ear to ear. She could hear her father's love in his new song.

"And with joy, they sang songs of happiness and love for God. The songs were filled with so much love that they changed the sad sound of the entire house to joy. The mother came quickly as she heard the joy of the major sound-fruit ringing.

And the mother joyfully sang, 'Praise be to God, surely goodness and mercy shall follow us all the days of our lives!' Selah."

The Song of a Warrior

"There once lived a man that was overwhelmed by thoughts of war. This was only natural, because he was a great warrior that had fought long and hard in the name of the king. Everyday of the war, this man sang the warrior's minor sound-fruit song because it is the sound of war; war is death and pain.

"When the war was over, the warrior returned home. But as he returned, he carried within his heart the song of war. This song of war did not fit with the sounds of peace in his home. Before the war, his family knew him by his peaceful song. But now his song had changed, and his family did not know him. The warrior man tried to sing his old songs of peace, but his heart was in tune with war and death.

"Then one day the warrior man went to church. But he did not go to just any church. He went to a church that sang true songs of praise to God. This was a church that knew the purpose and principles of Christian music. Sounds of a major sound-fruit were sung with the words of love, joy, and peace. He had not sung these songs in many moons. He was overcome by this music, and his heart began to change keys to the major sound-fruit of love. When the man returned home from the church, his family began to know him through the sound of love. Selah."

A silence filled the air as Percy closed his eyes and said, "Bashiri, I sense unforgiveness in your heart, and that unforgiveness is blocking your relationship with God. I hear your unforgiving heart in the song of your voice. But verily I say unto you; if you walk in forgiveness, your music will reach the gates of Heaven. Show your love through forgiveness. God hears the sound of love, because God is love."

Bashiri heard the words of Percy and was deeply moved. So Percy pointed towards the depth of the garden. There was a cave hidden deep within the trees. In excitement, Bashiri walked steadily to the cave. He was about to learn a great secret, as you are about to learn a great secret. Your mind is being prepared with every page of this ancient scroll. But first we must find out if Otto is still alive!

CHAPTER 5

THE COURT BECAME ANGRY as the crowd of my supporters grew more vocal. "Silence! Silence! I demand that the prisoner be brought forward!" yelled a judge of the Royal Court.

The doors of the royal court opened slowly, and there I was standing between two guards. The guards escorted me through the isles of the majestic court. As I approached the bench, one of the judges spoke to me in a most foul tone. "King Clef, ruler of the Kingdom of Mir, insists that you are a fake. The king believes that you are deceiving people with lies about Christian music principles. Therefore, you are charged with the crime of heresy! You have also spoken vehemently against our royal church music, therefore you are also charged with blasphemy!"

I replied in the most humble of tones. "I am but a humble servant of the Lord trying to spread the good news of God's music. Blasphemy and heresy are not dishes offered on the musical menu from which I serve. I am but a Disciples of Christian Music, a humble psalmist for the Lord."

"The king says that you are in possession of the Golden Tone! Is this true?" asked the Judge.

Not a whisper fell from the mouths of the onlookers; they were awaiting my answer. But the Golden Tone is a myth, a legend. Many people have sought after the Golden Tone for centuries. The legend comes from the story of David and Saul. If you read the 16th chapter of First Samuel, you will come across the story of Saul, the King of Israel before King David. During this time, the Spirit of the Lord had left King Saul and Saul became terrorized by evil spirits. But knowing well the power that God placed within music, the servants of the king sought out a skillful musician to play special music that would make King Saul well again. The skillful player was a young man named David (who would later become King of Israel and author of half of the Book of Psalms).

> *So it came about whenever the evil Spirit from God came to Saul, David would take the harp and play it with his hand; and Saul would be refreshed and be well, and the evil spirits would depart from him.*

> I Samuel 16:23

David was able to produce the most beautiful and meaningful sounds from his harp. This music drove the evil spirits out of the king. Some people believed that this music had a special sound, a tone, that had the power to heal all sickness. Some people even started to believe that this gold-like tone should be worshipped. Many adventurous people have searched the known world for this Golden Tone, yet none have found it. It remains a mystery.

"Are you the bearer of the secret Golden Tone?" the judge yelled in anger, "King Clef has been told about all of the powers of the Golden Tone: the tone that calms the savage beast, the tone that cast out evil spirits. Is this true? Are you in possession of the Golden Tone?"

I looked into the eyes of the judge, smiled, and calmly replied, "Yes."

"The king demands to know the secret you possess, or your head will roll when the rooster crows!" demanded the court.

With peace I replied, "I mean no harm and speak no evil. Let me have a chance to plead my case. You need to know why the golden tone is a secret before you possess it or else it will overtake the kingdom. Please allow me to break the bread of knowledge with the chief musician of your kingdom. If he is not truly satisfied with my words, I will gladly hand over the Golden Tone and leave the city vowing never to return. But if you allow me to explain the Golden Tone's music to you, I promise that you will have a musical experience so spiritual that you will praise the name of the Lord from now until the second coming!"

"We will ask the king." And under the judge's orders, the messenger took my request to the king.

After a short time, the messenger returned with a scroll closed with the royal seal. The judges broke the seal and proclaimed king's decree. "I, King Clef, order Otto to challenge the Chief Musician in a musical debate."

CHAPTER 6

BASHIRI BEGAN TO WALK through the thick bushes of the garden until he reached the cave. Upon entering the dark cave, Bashiri saw the book marked SELAH on an old table. He ran towards the book in excitement; he was so happy! "I will finally know God's Law of Sound. Let me get the book and leave this cave before the day changes to night."

As Bashiri picked up the book, he heard a loud click. Suddenly, a hidden stone door fell in front of the cave. The falling door sparked a flint stone that sat next to an oil lamp. The lamp then filled the cave with a bright light. Bashiri realized that he was trapped with the book marked SELAH in his hands. His heart filled with fear.

"I cannot believe it. There was a table-trigger under this book, and now I am trapped in this cave. But wait! What is written on the door?" He looked at the faint letters covered in dust and spider webs:

LEARN GOD'S LAW OF SOUND
OR YE SHALL NEVER BE FOUND

The fear of the angel of death ran through Bashiri's chest. He searched the room high and low for a way to escape the cave. That was when he found an inscription on the wall at the back of the cave. The inscription spelled out the word, SELAH. "What does this SELAH mean? And these shapes below the SELAH are nothing but triangles."

And with a celestial ray of light, the Spirit of the Lord opened great revelations in Bashiri's mind. The Lord began to reveal a musical truth about the War in Heaven. "I see now, oh Lord, the vision of music. Who went to war against God in Heaven? It was Satan and a third of the angels. What was Satan's job in Heaven? He was the Chief Musician, Leader of Praise and Worship, The Anointed Cherub (Ezekiel 28:14). So this means that angels joined the rebelling Minister of Music in Heaven.

"The Minister of Music wanted to become God. Oh my, the War in Heaven was against God and the Minister of Music! The original sin, the rebellion against God, was committed by the Minister of Music! That is why music is so important to the church!"

Bashiri paused for a moment to meditate on the magnitude of this revelation. "That is why the Devil uses music against people. Being a minister of music is the highest form of life that Satan has ever known. Satan is the Great Deceiver of what he is best at, music." The reality of Bashiri's mortality began to sink in.

"There has to be a way out of this cave!" he shouted as he investigated the room for an exit. It was at that time that he noticed a message on the trigger where the book sat:

OVERTONE

UNDERTONE

SELAH

"What does it mean?" he thought, "Overtone and Undertone; this must be a musical clue to my freedom." So Bashiri opened the book and began to read for his life. Racing page by page, he learned more of the secrets of music, the programming of the mind, and the shapes of sound. In amazement he thought, "I cannot believe my eyes! The triangles, the reversing pyramids, Music and the Star of David, this book is truly amazing! Now, how can these symbols free me from this cave!" His frustrations began to set in as the revelations stopped.

CHAPTER 7

THE KING POUNDED HIS fist on the table in anger. King Clef was a man skilled in the art of controlling people. But he knew that if he had me killed, the people of the kingdom might have thought that the king feared my knowledge. So he agreed to have the wisest musician challenge me.

"I am Jengo, the Chief Musician here in the Kingdom of Mir. There is nothing of music that I do not know. I am here to challenge your knowledge of music and take the Golden Tone from you!" he announced.

With confidence and a smile, I replied, "Let us begin with an agreement. One thing that we all can agree on is that music has the ability to take you to another world. When you are in the church, the music can help you forget about your problems. But what if the musician in charge likes the power of being able to control your musical world? The church musician can make your world happy or sad with the change of a sound-fruit. The musician has the power to direct the emotions of the listener. Is that not power; does not power come with responsibility?

"Now let me ask you a question, Jengo. Are some of your musicians trying to play God? Are the lives of your musicians so out of control that they want to take everyone into a musical world that they control? Do your musicians have a God complex? Are they in need of repentance? If you are one of those musicians, should you not fall to your knees and repent?" (Even now as you are reading this scroll, you may need to bow your head and repent).

"I have no God-complex! I am a man of the Bible," Jengo replied in anger.

I responded in a most apologetic tone. "I mean no disrespect. I am honored by your presence. You are no doubt a skilled musician deficient of no musical knowledge. Now, let me ask you a question. Does God desire to be praised with the major sound-fruit or the minor sound-fruit?"

"God is fair so He loves all truth and all music," arrogantly exclaimed Jengo.

I kindly asked, "Well, even though God loves you, does He desire the good in you or the evil? Would it not be the good, and is that not the real truth? Besides, music was created to glorify God, was it not?"

"I suppose this is true," answered Jengo.

"And does not the truth involve both good and evil?" I asked.

Jengo replied in a grumbling voice, "Yes. The truth does involve them both."

"So would it be better to glorify God with good or evil?" I asked.

"If we are to glorify God, it must be with good!" said Jengo in a stately manner.

I felt the hand of God at work as I continued, "Then can we agree that the music that God wants us to glorify Him with must be the music of good."

Jengo peacefully replied, "On this, we can agree."

"Good, good, good!" I said as I smiled and clapped my hands. "Now back to my original question. Does God desire to be praised with the major sound-fruit or the minor sound-fruit?"

"Well, who is to say?" Jengo asked.

I smiled and asked, "Well, do all of the people in the land agree that the major sound-fruit holds within it the sounds of good, victory, love, and joy?

Jengo peacefully replied, "On this, we all agree."

I continued, "And do not all of these people agree that the minor sound-fruit holds within it the sound of suffering, trials, pain, and war?"

"Yes, this is undeniable," remarked Jengo.

"And although in music, like in man, there can be good and evil, does not both good and evil represent the whole truth of music?" I asked.

"Yes, it does represent the whole truth of music," Jengo agreed in hesitation.

"And if God desires anything of us, would it be good or evil?" I courageously asked.

"If God desires anything from us, it would be that which is good. God desires our best!" Jengo said in amazement.

"And are not the qualities of good held within the major sound-fruit?" I asked.

"Yes!" the court replied in unison.

"Then would not the major sound-fruit be the sound of praise that God desires?" I shouted across the room.

"Yes, yes this is true. Oh thank you for coming to this kingdom. I am truly humbled," announced Jengo.

I rejoiced. "Your ears are now open. My dear friends, the minor sound-fruit can be useful to help us remember the pain of life, but it can also root us in pain if that pain becomes the root of our music. The minor sound-fruit tells us about pain and fighting, but it is not glorifying God. Do you know what you get if you play a minor sad song backwards? You get your major sound back, you get your family back, you get your hope back, and you get your faith back!

"The Minor sound-fruit represents a good life in reverse. My prayer is for the minor sound-fruit to be used to show you what God has brought you out of. My friend, music is neither good nor evil. Music is a force that can be used in good and evil ways. But praise is a house built on the foundation of the major sound-fruit.

"The Bible contains many examples of evil, such as: trials, hate, and Satan's trickery. But the Bible does not rejoice in those examples. The Bible rejoices in the victory, the love, and the mercy of God. Be careful not to live in your trials. Be careful not to live in the valley of the shadow of death. Be careful not to live on a diet of minor sound-fruit. For the Bible says in the 23rd chapter of The Psalms, '*Ye though I walk* **through** *the Valley of the Shadow of Death, I shall fear no evil*'.

"The scripture does not say that we shall live in the valley, but to walk through it. The Valley of the Shadow of Death has the sound of the minor sound-fruit. So walk through minor sound-fruit. Be not afraid of evil; yet do not rejoice in it by building a house on a foundation of minor sound-fruit. Learn from the valleys and hardships in your life and live with your hand reaching out to the right hand of the Almighty God that can pull you out of the valley.

"And do all things decent and in order. To raise the spirit with words and lower the spirit with minor sound-fruit is to serve two different masters and is out of order. To serve two masters means that there are two heads with opposing minds, and anything with two heads is a beast. If the music and the words are traveling in opposite directions, the music is a two-headed beast. This beast is the author of confusion and is not of God. The Bible even tells us that 'God is not the author of confusion' (I Corinthians 14:33).

"So learn to see God working in every situation. Seek not the Golden Tone, but worship God with the major sound-fruit. If the major sound-fruit raises the spirit, then edify people with the major sound-fruit.

"God is love and love is the great commission of Jesus Christ. Your music should be filled will the great commission in spirit and in truth. Your music should be filled with the major sound-fruit. Your music should be filled with love. Let us pray."And with that, the entire court took to their knees in prayer.

Observing from a hidden room in the courthouse was an evil shadow. The shadow turned to his servant that smiled at the words of Otto. And with the strings of his harp, the mysterious shadow played the song of a minor sound-fruit until the servant was never more, never more.

CHAPTER 8

THE DISCIPLES OF CHRISTIAN Music knew well that the chances of reclaiming my freedom had grown slim. My success in the courtroom had angered the king. The king had let his anger be known by releasing the henchman's song of vengeance, The Song of the Axe Man (the axe-man cometh on the second day of the month). My death had been ordered. So the time had come for me to pass the final secrets of music along to my students.

So I sent word for my students to gather at the Royal Jail. I spoke to them as only a serious teacher could. "You all have been the best disciples that I could have ever hoped for. You have cherished some of the most important lessons in music since I taught you about Music in the Garden of Good and Evil:

The Meaning of the Sound-Fruit
The Doctrine of Sound Combination
The Ten Tablets and the Parables
The Nature of Man and Music
The Principle of Sound/Word Alignment

All of you have been faithful to the three principles:

Be Ye Led By The Spirit
Be Ye Rooted in Christ
Be Ye Wise in Musical Knowledge

And all of you have been committed to God's purpose for music:

To Glorify God and to Edify Man

"But I feel a divide in the world that you all must destroy. I am nearing the end of my life, and I am no longer able to carry out the last mission. The name of this mission is: THE GREAT WALL OF CHRISTIAN MUSIC.

"There is much division in the world of Christian music. A great wall exist between the people of traditional and contemporary music. This wall divides the church into two empires of thinking. This is a wall built in the minds of Christians. If this wall is not destroyed, the most unthinkable events will unfold. The children will turn against their parents. The young will turn against the elderly. This division will then lead to a war between the empires. They will call it 'THE WAR TO END ALL WARS', and the empires will strike back at one another."

The Disciples stood in shock. This wall was indestructible, impenetrable, the most... Well, you get the picture. China built a great big wall just like it.

One of the disciple, Safina, spoke about this epic mission that the disciples had been charged with. With her voice full of doubt and fear, Safina cried out, "Otto, listen to what you are saying. Us, destroy a wall with no weapons, no metal axes, no---"

"Oh ye of little faith," I gently said to Safina, "Do you not remember the story about the Wall of Jericho? To God, what is a wall of brick and mortar? Nothing is impossible for God, but some things are impossible without faith. Faith is when you believe, talk, and act because God's word is true".

"But how can you expect me to have faith when the courts are treating you so unfairly!" she shouted. Puddles began to gather in the wells of her eyes.

I saw that she was angry; her mind had lost its reason. Safina's anger and sadness had blown out her lamp of reason. So I placed my arm between the cold prison bars and touched her shoulder to comfort her. "Was not our Savior, Jesus Christ, treated unfairly when his life was taken. God's only begotten Son did not even get a fair trial. So why should I, a mere servant of God, think that I am entitled to a fair trial from the courts of man? Did not the Bible tell us in Matthew 26:62-68 that Jesus faced unfair treatment? So be encouraged. When life is unfair, you can trust God to do what is right."

Her heart was calmed; her sad song brightened to

a major key. I looked back at the disciples and continued. "Lastly, I want to talk about your emotions. You can stop your actions but not your emotions! You can only stop your emotions from affecting your actions. Also remember, you cannot argue with music. You cannot out-think, out-logic, or out-run music. You cannot reason with it or plead for its mercy.

"The effects of music can overtake you fast like a sandstorm or slow like an hourglass. Music travels straight to your emotions like a witch's brew attacking the heart. Music travels pass the unguarded gates of the mind straight into your soul. And even if your gate is guarded, your mind is still vulnerable like a man using a wooden fence to keep the wind out of his yard. You cannot block sound with open ears. God did not design us that way. God made us hear.

"Words act upon your intellect and may or may not affect your emotions. But music acts upon your emotions and may or may not enter the intellect. You may never know that the music of a minor sound-fruit has affected you until the day you just find yourself living a sad life. At that point, your spirit will have become a minor sound-fruit spirit. So know that we are not human beings having spiritual experiences; we are spiritual beings having human experiences. You should not be ruled by your fleshly emotions... but now tell me, has anyone heard from Bashiri?"

CHAPTER 9

BASHIRI WAS IN A world of amazement, but he knew that he had to keep reading to make it out of the cave alive. And in the book marked SELAH, it was written:

The tongue is a mighty pen, and we write on the tablets of our heart (Proverbs 3:3-4). Songs ingrain messages in your heart like a gardener plants seeds. The Song of Moses was God's way of planting a seed in the minds of Israel. Even Moses, on his deathbed, knew the power of music. Music was the one thing that could carry God's commands from generation to generation for thousands of years. Deuteronomy 31:19, 21-22 says:

> *19 Now therefore write ye this song for you, and teach it (to) the children of Israel: put it in their mouths, that this song may be a witness for me against the children of Israel.*
>
> *21 And it shall come to pass, when many evils and troubles are befallen them, that this song shall testify against them as a witness; for it shall not be forgotten out of the mouths of their seed...*

22 Moses therefore wrote this song the same day, and taught it (to) the children of Israel.

Music was so important to the salvation of Israel that when Moses finished writing the song into a book, he ordered the Levites to place the song into the Ark of the Covenant (Deuteronomy 31:26)

"The power within music was so strong that God choose a song to save a generation that was doomed to become wicked. Music was so important that Moses had this song placed in the Ark of the Covenant."

Bursts of light filled the eyes of Bashiri. A vision appeared; sound appeared in a vision! Sound like this had never been seen before, only the sound-fruit. But now the vision of sound filled his mind's eye. He put the revelation into practice in the cave and recorded the vision on scrolls that he found on the table.

The first revelation was that of the ringing hammers. A metal hammer beating on more metal could be heard ringing throughout the cave. Within the ringing, Bashiri heard more hammers and more ringing. The sounds were overwhelming but clear in intent.

"The hammers must have been activated by the movement of the book. But the tones are different. Why do they sound so different from one another?" Bashiri thought.

He looked on the table were the book once sat and saw hammers that appeared from nowhere. Bashiri was shocked, but he continued. Then a wonderous pattern began to emerge in his mind. He noticed that the hammers were of definite sizes; each one was half the size of the last one. "A ratio is what I hear and see, a mathematical ratio. The sounds fit harmoniously within one another. These sounds must be connected by God's Law of Sound."

Soon he began to experiment with the hammers and discovered that the sounds became higher in pitch like chirping birds as the hammers became smaller. He recorded the ratios of sound as 2:1, 3:2, 4:3, and so on. After careful calculations, Bashiri made a fascinating discovery. He found that if he hit all of the hammers at the same time, he would hear the same sounds that the ringing of the first hammer made by itself. What was discovered stunned him. "I can hear the sounds in the metal. My God, I hear a major sound-fruit, the sound of peace. The natural ringing of metal objects creates the major sound of love, joy, and peace!"

He began to hit other objects in the cave. "The same thing happens with everything I strike. One sound is closely related to other sounds that are higher in pitch and ascending to Heaven. This is the ringing sound that I hear. This is the glow that surrounds a sound-fruit. This is what makes a voice sound beautiful. The ringing of sound has the message of love, joy, and peace embedded within it. This is the overtone. Now what is an undertone?"

Bashiri found that if an overtone was the sound

happiness, the sound for sadness must be the opposite of happiness. So he created a mathematical model in which a line represented the foundation of musical sound (the fundamental). He then had a revelation of the divine number of seven. So Bashiri took the first three overtones from three levels of sounds and created his seven-letter scale (the *Do-Ra-Me* scale).

"God created the world in seven days and each day had its own sound. And just as the stars sang together in the creation of the universe (Job 38:7), so did the sounds of three musical overtones come together to make the seven-note scale. Now, the overtones of the sound that we call 'C' are C-C-G-C-E, (the octave, the perfect 5th, the perfect 4th, and the Major 3rd). Placed within the divine order of three, the notes form the sound of a major sound-fruit (a major chord). This is the sound of love, joy, peace, and victory!

"Now I shall draw the vision of the sound. If I mathematically plot a representation of the sound, I will then see three levels of sound; I will see a sound built on the divine number, three. So, first I will create a graph to plot the major sound:

.   . Minor 3rd

.   . Major 3rd

——————— Foundation

"Now, the distance between the base of the sound and the third level of sound is the foundation of the sound. So the foundation is a major third, the sound will be a major sound. I wonder what shape would be created if I connected the three levels of sound to a point:

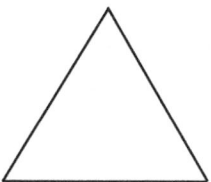

"It is a perfect triangle pointing towards Heaven. This sound lifts the soul up like chariots of fire. Amazing! The major sound-fruit points toward Heaven. Love, joy, peace and victory; this is the beginning of God's Law of Sound."

Excited to learn more, Bashiri dove deeper into the book until he reached the page marked 'Sorrow and Pain'. Under those words was the message 'Minor Sound-Fruit'. Now, Bashiri knew from his studies that the minor sound-fruit was used for pain, suffering, war, and death. But what came next he was not ready for (Reader, PLEASE PAY CLOSE ATTENTION).

The word, undertone, was written below the words of war and death. But there was another mysterious message below undertone. Those words struck a chord of fear is Bashiri's heart.

REVERSE THE SYMBOLS,
DRAW SORROW FROM THE WELL,
REVERSE THE SYMBOLS,
DRAW YOUR SOUL INTO HELL!

Below was a triangle that pointed down representing the minor sound-fruit. Inside of the triangle was the figure of a man crying out in pain. Bashiri was in shock and awe because of the truths that had crossed his eyes.

Then Bashiri turned to the next page and became terrified at what he saw. His eyes stumbled onto a secret more shocking than the first. He dropped the book and ran to the corner of the cave. "The secrets, Percy said that they would be too much. I must forget what I am seeing! I must forget!"

Bashiri saw the parallel forces of music in opposition. He saw the triangles, the pyramids, reversed against one another. He saw the STAR OF DAVID!

CHAPTER 10

BASHIRI FORCED HIMSELF TO gaze upon the Star of David. "My God, this shape is of the two directions of music; joy is rising out of pain! The major sound-fruit raises the soul up and the minor sound-fruit pulls the soul down. No one would believe me if I told them about these shapes."

So Bashiri used his skills of math to set these sounds of music to measurements. The collections of sounds were set to a straight line of a graph. He then found that the sounds of all sound-fruit were built upon the divine number of three. So starting with the major sound-fruit, he marked the points on the scroll three spaces above the original line. "I see, now! There are major and minor qualities of this sound. It is the root (foundation) of the sound that will tell me if the sound is of joy or pain. Okay, this first measurement above the foundation will represent the shape of a major sound. It will represent the major foundation above the root of the sound.

"This first level will be called a major third. The next level (third) shows that the minor is not the

49

foundation but is separated from the root of the sound by the peace and joy of the major third. The triangle points up towards Heaven just as the major sound-fruit lifts your spirits. The major foundation of sound conquers over the minor. These measurements confirm that the major sound-fruit is part of God's Law of Sound."

Bashiri then reversed the coordinates of the major sound-fruit, and the triangle pointed down towards hell; the minor sound-fruit pulls your spirit down. Bashiri spoke to himself in the cave, "It pulls your spirit down like when you are swimming in the sea, and you feel something grabbing your leg and pulling you down." Then Bashiri's ambition turned to anger. "Like when my little brother cried out to God as he was being pulled down in the sea. I am still angry with God. God turned His back on my brother? Where was God then?"

But then the voice of God spoke to Bashiri's heart. "My Son, I did not rescue your brother from drowning on that day, but I did reached down My hand and saved your brother's soul." Bashiri wept. He was comforted by the words of the Lord. Tears of peace ran down his face; he had let go of his pain.

So Bashiri gathered his tears and returned to work. "The measurements confirm the secret of the minor sound-fruit. The measurements confirm that the opposite coordinates change the sound from major to minor, from joy to pain, from peace to war, and from victory to defeat. But Jesus came and brought the world from defeat to victory, from war to peace, from pain to joy, and from death to life! Glory be to God!" Then Bashiri broke out into a praise of tears.

As Bashiri shouted for joy, the spirit of praise filled his heart like a mighty rushing river would fill a cup; his cup had runneth over. Bashiri rejoiced because God had given him peace about his brother's death. God gave Bashiri a peace that his heart had not room to receive.

"I can cry because Jesus wept and I can dance because David danced! Oh Jesus!" And Bashiri began to cry tears of joy and praised the name of the Lord for saving his brother's soul. The tears ran down his face. Bashiri fell to the floor; he was slain in the spirit. "I see your face, my brother, and your soul has been saved." The bitterness and unforgiveness Bashiri held for God was replaced by love and understanding.

After Bashiri praised the name of the Lord, he looked at the graph for one final calculation. "One triangle points up and the opposite joins together as a reverse triangle. The measurements form the Star of David! It is true! Praise is rising towards Heaven through the minor sound of hardship. It is a sign of victory. This is God's Law of Sound!"

CHAPTER 11

KING CLEF HELD HIS head down in fearful contemplation, "I do not know what I will do if the Golden Tone is not in my possession. The Shadow helped me become king; soon he will come to collect on the debt. If I do not deliver the Golden Tone to the Shadow, my life will surely be over. I do not know ---" A messenger interrupted the king's train of thought.

"You have a visitor," the messenger announced.

"Not now, send him away!" the king shouted.

"My king, I would have sent him away. But you said that you are never to be interrupted unless it was The Shadow, and well...it's The Shadow," the messenger timidly replied.

Fear filled every corner of the king's heart upon hearing the messenger's announcement, but still he hurried to see the Shadow. As the king entered the main room, a heat had overtaken his body; the pain of a thousand needles manifested in his chest.

"Shadow", the king said while clutching his chest in pain, "to what do I owe the honor of your visit?"

The only part of the Shadow that you could see

was his blood-filled eyes like those of a rotting fish. The Shadow spoke in a low, angered tone. "I cannot believe you let Otto gain the support of your chief musician. Not once since I was cast down from grace had I witnessed such a defeat. I am glad to know that I am not the only failure in the room. But as my failures have made me stronger, your failures are threatening your life. I am the one that will bring death upon you faster than you can bring it upon yourself!" screamed the Shadow.

"Yes, I know but...oh...the pain! Please make it stop!" cried the king. And with a snap of the Shadow's fingers, the king's pain stopped. "Who are you? You must tell me!" begged the king.

"Oh, I go by so many names, but it has been a long time since I have been by called my given name. Some people call me Satan. I am the blood moon of the noonday sun. Some people call me the devil. Remove the 'D' and you have evil. If you spell it backwards, *evil* becomes *live*, fa la-la la-la," sang the Shadow. He was like a laughing madman, and like a madman he jumped from one corner of the room to the next in clouds of smoke.

"They even call me Lucifer, The Light-Bearer. Now that's just funny. Oh people, please stop the violence; your ignorance is killing me!" he laughed. "My favorite name is the 'anointed cherub'; for at one time I was the Chief Musician in Heaven. I go by so many names, but you can call me Dad." A sinister laugh crept from the bellows of Satan; the king trembled in fear at the evil that stood before him.

"I am the whisper in her ear saying, 'He does not love you, so jump my dear.' I am the great deceiver, the dealer of death, the devourer that seeketh a Christian's last breath. I have a plan to control the people. But I must know the that true golden tone has been destroyed; then the world will be mine. Now, I am not able to touch the Golden Tone, but you can bury it. Get the Golden Tone, bury it deep within the earth and bring me Otto. You have one week." Satan disappeared in a cloud of smoke leaving the King to do his bidding.

CHAPTER 12

THE KING ENTERED THE jail and shouted at me with a blade to my throat. "I demand to know the location of the Golden Tone!"

I looked at the king ever so peacefully and gently replied, "This is a simple matter. The Golden Tone is kept in the Garden of Good and Evil. But you cannot find it. The Golden Tone is a fruit that can only be seen by the pure of heart, yet it can be heard over a thousand mountaintops. Now please, put down your blade. My throat is no closer to the Golden Tone than you are."

King Clef dropped his blade and left in frustration. He returned back to his chambers where the Shadow again appeared out of a cloud of smoke.

"I overheard the words of Otto. I am angry, but I have a thought. With Otto in jail, you now have the chance to create something new, a new religion! You will be crowned with a new title, THE SOUND KING! Your royal subjects will praise you in sound," spoke the Shadow into the king's ear. You could here this silver-tongued snake hissing the sales-pitch.

The king's eyes grew as big as elephant ears. "I can see it. The people will worship an image of sound, a golden tone! Yes, we will create our very own golden tone. Oh, Lucifer, you are brilliant, you are..." the king suddenly noticed that Satan was no longer in the room. "Guards, bring me the Royal Ministry!"

The ministers all gathered in the king's chambers and learned of Satan's devilish plans for a new religion. Then the king ordered a Golden Tone to be made and worshipped by all.

"Do you want us to place the image in front of the church?" a minister asked.

"No! Destroy the church and put the Golden Tone in its place," the king declared.

"What should this graven image look like?" a minister asked.

"I got it!" a royal musician exclaimed, "Fashion it into the shape of something that the people trust. The idol is a tone, and a tone is a sound that has been shaped for a purpose. So let us create the Golden Tone in the image of a golden sound-fruit. We can make it the height of ten men and just as wide!"

"Brilliant! Brilliant! Brilliant!" The Royal Ministry shouted in agreement.

And it was in that room that the plans for the new religion were shaped. A tax was levied against the kingdom to collect the gold needed to build the graven image. It was called "THE RELIGION OF

HOPE TAX". This tax also provided money for musicians and sound-fruit so that the music of the Golden Tone could play a never-ending song.

And it was so. The people of the kingdom were told that their lives were hard because God had turned His back on them. The church was then destroyed without rebellion from the people. But then their lives became even more difficult. It was the taxes that were making their lives so hard, not God. So the "THE RELIGION OF HOPE TAX" was then renamed a "Tithe". So then it came to pass that the people of the Kingdom of Mir felt good about tithing to the Golden Tone.

And the people saw the Golden Tone and were impressed by its beauty. Then when the people heard its music, the people were overtaken by feelings of lust and greed. Special chants and songs secretly composed by Satan were sung to the Golden Tone. Satan had cleverly created chants that secretly carried messages of the seven deadly sins: lust, gluttony, greed, sloth, wrath, envy, and pride. By singing these songs, the people trained their hearts with the same sounds that Satan composed for Sodom and Gomorrah.

And it came to pass that whenever the people sang, evil spirits were summoned to the soul of the listener. Music became the open door that invited evil spirits into the soul. The more that Satan composed, the more the souls of the people decomposed.

Where the word of God once dwelt, now dwelt the song of evil. The song of the Golden Tone spoke against Christ. This was the antichrist!

And every spirit that confesseth not that Jesus Christ is come in the flesh is not of God: and this is that spirit of antichrist.

I John 4:3

Satan knew the Bible well. He thought, "*The tongue is a mighty pen and we write on the tablets of our heart.* Proverbs 3:3-4! I am so glad that the people do not know the word of God like I do. Music can talk to the ever-listening soul, while the mind stays deaf. It reminds me of the good old days of Moses in the Mountain and a so-called chosen people gone astray." Satan laughed a devilish laugh and grinned a devilish grin. When souls are lost, his joy begins.

All of the while, I sat in the jail thinking about the scripture, "*My people are destroyed for lack of knowledge*" (Hosea 4:6). The people have now been lead astray with autosuggestion, the programming of the mind. I spoke to the disciples about this trickery! My heart cried tears of lament for the scattered souls of the kingdom. My heart sang the minor sound-fruit of woe and despair.

CHAPTER 13

THE SUN ROSE WITH PATIENCE over the Adili Mountains of the east. It was morning time, and the disciples had come to visit me. I asked them a morning query. "Have you heard of the Sound of Death?"

"No, this is not known to our lands," said one of the disciples.

I then took a deep breath and spoke in caution. "The Sound of Death comes from Satan's attempt to play God. After being thrown out of God's presence in Heaven, the great deceiver set out to build a garden of sound that would compare to the beauty of the Garden of Good and Evil. But the only thing that Satan was able to grow were rows of rotten sound-fruit. These rotten fruit made sounds of constant pain and wickedness.

"The stench from Satan's garden was so bad that pigs and maggots would not eat from it. The Devil soon found out that he could only produce a garden as good as his was. Since Satan was no good, neither were his fruit. And since Satan was rotten to the core, so were the fruit of his Garden. His very best was corrupt; his very best was rotten. His very best fruit was dead to the core; therefore, the only sound that Satan could produce was *The Sound of Death!*"

"What does it sound like? What does his garden look like? Where is his garden?" everyone asked in a tone of fear.

"Jesus said in Matthew 7:16 that '*Ye shall know them by their fruit*'. So where is Satan's Forbidden Garden of Death? It is in a valley. Where is the valley that nobody dares to go? The Bible does give us the location as a musical clue in the Book of Psalms," I stated.

The disciples wrestled open there Bibles to find the scripture when one of the disciples shouted, "I got it, Psalm 23:4, The Valley of the Shadow of Death!"

"That is correct, Safina! I first encountered this valley on my way to the Garden of Good and Evil. The Forbidden Garden of Death was a very scary garden, indeed. I heard so many strange sounds of horror that I dared not stop. The sounds from Satan's garden made me sick and angry.

"That is why the Bible tells us to walk through the Valley of the Shadow of Death instead of to live in it. This forbidden garden had every deadly sound of Satan. Every tree in his garden had evil snake roots. Corrupt were Satan's trees, and Jesus warns us that '*a corrupt tree bringeth forth evil fruit*' (Matthew 7:17).

"The Forbidden Garden of Death has a gardener that plants vines of sound that grow around the minds of the partakers of the rotten sound-fruit. Next, the strangling vines give the listeners a slow spiritual death, until only the mind and body are left. This evil garden also has a messenger of golden music. He has the power to disguise the sound of death as sweet music and feed it to people.

"So the devil has two weapons. He seduces musicians to use music in strange ways that take the glory away from God. But the Devil also has a weapon of sound to bring forth death and destruction. He will come as a blood-moon shadow blocking the light of God. And those that listen to his music will be made deaf to the voice of God."

It was at this time that a woman came to the jail searching for me. She was full of fear and confusion. I heard the fear of the minor sound-fruit in her trembling voice as she called my name. I heard the torment of the diminished sound-fruit in her words. Listen to her story.

"My dear lady, peace be unto you. How might I be of service?" I asked.

Trying to catch her breath, she cried out, "My son, my son! In the night, my son gave himself over to the sounds of an evil golden piper. I knew the thing was evil because my son sang a new song that glorified the disrespect of women, the love of fornication, and the rebellion of the youth!" At that point, her voice turned to anger because she knew that these songs were an abomination to God.

So I spoke to the mother about of the evil weapons of Satan. "The king is using his new religion to change the song of the youth. But this song sounds more like the handiwork of Satan. Satan has a demon, a Golden Piper, capable of seducing children with sinful music, sweet like chocolate. Now, all of you must learn this lesson as God is revealing it to me. Write it on a scroll so that it may be remembered.

The Speaking Scroll

"We all speak in song! The Bible tells of this in Ephesians 5:19 when Paul said that we should all be '*Speaking to (one another) in psalms and hymns and spiritual songs...*' God created us to speak in song, and He tells us the specific songs to speak in: psalms and hymns, and spiritual songs. Listen to my voice. Am I not speaking in tones? Have you not heard a speaker that was boring to listen to because he had a flat and lifeless voice? When you heard this, did you not say that the speaker had a 'monotone' voice?

"The word mono-tone means that there is only one musical sound being brought forth. But when that voice rises and falls and pauses with accents, this is a voice that people pay attention to! This person is speaking in different tones of musical sound. This is a person speaking in song. When people are happy, their voices make certain sounds. Their voices become pleasing and cause the people around them to be happy as well. Then every voice takes on a happy tone.

"But have you heard a depressed person speak and suddenly you felt depressed? What happened was that you got in tune with the depressed person's song. His song became your song. Satan also uses music to change the song of your life. Satan will use his song to draw out the sin buried deep within you. If your song of sin becomes louder than your song of praise, then Satan has turned you away from God."

I then turned to the mother and said, "Do you remember a warning about this in the Bible? In Mark 4:24, Jesus said, '*take heed of what you listen to*'. The word, heed, is a warning. We must be sure to guard our ears from Satan's music. Now, Satan has changed your son's song, but we can combat this evil. The Bible tells us how to overcome Satan's musical hold. The word of God tells us to follow the instructions given in Ephesians 5:19. You must speak to your son in psalms, hymns, and spirituals songs."

I then focused my attention back on the eager disciples. "Now, let us speak of the spiritual gifts of this kingdom. This kingdom is full of gifted musicians that God wants to use. But they do not want to be ministers of music. They want to make the music they like but are not willing to surrender their music for the worship of God. Now they have passed their curse of disobedience onto the youth.

"God wanted to use the musicians of the king-dom, but the musicians told God that they were not willing to be musical servants. That meant that these musicians loved God only to that musical point and no farther. But when they stop telling God what they will and will not do, then God can use them. But they might want to be careful; *The Lord giveth and the Lord taketh away* (Job 1:31).

"The children are being taken away, but your faith and works can bring them back. Dear lady, to save your son you must let out a mighty song of praise to the Lord!"

CHAPTER 14

IN THE CAVE, THE Lord saw the tears rolling down Bashiri's face. God saw that Bashiri had become as clay for the Potter; God knew that now Bashiri's heart could be molded and was now rooted in Christ. And the Lord spoke to Bashiri saying, "I shall now remove the thorn from your flesh. I put it there as a messenger of Satan to torment you so that you would not exalt yourself through your music (II Corinthians 12:7). So from this day forth, you shall be known by a new name, Selah (meaning a musical interlude in which you pause and meditate on the word of the Lord).

"You will be the one who makes people pause and think about My purpose for music. You now know the truth, and the truth has set you free. Go forth from this cave and share this revelation, so that My music will live in the hearts of Christians!" And a beautiful angel of the Lord descended from Heaven and rolled away the stone door from the cave.

Bashiri emerged from the cave as Selah; a new musical butterfly released from a cocoon to soar above the earth. He had been transformed by the renewal of his mind (Romans 12:2). The Potter had shaped Selah's mind to do Kingdom work. God had given him the Law of Sound to redeem a kingdom that had fallen lower than the curse of the crawling snake (Genesis 3:14); the corrupt kingdom had become a distant cousin of Sodom and Gomorrah.

When Percy saw the face of Selah, he knew the Lord had made the student ready. "By the prophecy, you are Selah. You are now ready. You will walk where there are no floors, like Peter running on water to Jesus. Love where there is no love, because God is Love. Bring a song of praise to the self-singing world; for the Bible tells us to sing a new song. God is the same yesterday, today, and tomorrow. So God's law for music will remain the same from now to the ever after!

"If people are to make the right choice, they must know God's purpose for music. Jesus is the rock that the music ministry is to be built upon, and the Disciples of Christian Music are the rebuilders of the music ministry. Remember the purpose of music:

TO GLORIFY GOD AND TO EDIFY MAN

Remember the three main principles of Christian Music:

Be Ye Led By the Spirit
Be Ye Rooted in Christ
Be Ye Wise in Musical Knowledge

"And in the immortal words of Jesus Christ as recorded in Matthew 10:16, '*Behold, I send you forth as sheep in the midst of wolves: be ye therefore wise as serpents, and harmless as doves.*' This Golden Tone is but a Tower of Babel, no stronger than the Walls of Jericho. The Fruit of the Spirit shall break the yoke and shatter its walls. Take, therefore, this Fruit of the Spirit from the Tree of the Knowledge of Good and Evil. Use it to free the people of God from Satan's musical hold."

Percy placed the beautiful Fruit of the Spirit in the hands of Selah. Then Percy anointed Selah's head with oil and prayed the Lord's Prayer. And holding in his mind the revelation of music, Selah traveled back to the Kingdom of Mir.

CHAPTER 15

BACK AT THE CASTLE, Satan began to reposition himself. "King Clef, I really love this kingdom. I have so much fun turning Christian souls upside down," said Satan, with a sinister laugh. "I find it so easy to deceive the church people with music. I just give them a pretty sound hear and a taboo sound there. And like magic, their childish minds follow my music just like a dog follows his master. Yes, I am their master. Since I, Satan, could not be God in Heaven, I will become God on earth. Since I could not tempt Jesus in the wilderness, I tempted Judas in temple. And since I cannot kill Christian music, I will lace the music with sweet poisonous harmonies. And with every little sound of iniquity in the music of the church, evil is invited deeper into their souls."

"I feel like I am at a wedding because of all of these invitations. A new Christian soul is marrying my harlot daughter, Musica Temptress? What should I get these newlyweds? Hmmm, what to get, what to get? Silly me, I am not attending a marriage but rather a funeral. And this funeral is nothing other than an illicit affair between man and death. Now is the time to kill the spirit-man, and I love to start with the young." Satan spoke these words to the king with a silver-forked tongue. So smooth were the tones of his words; so musical were his thoughts.

The king was very impressed by the plan of the great Deceiver. "Shadow, how can I truly control the people?"

"First, you must make them come to you. Plant a seed to make them ask questions that you already know the answer to. Like I just did with you." Satan's smile was sinister like that of a jackal in the night. "You must build a hunger out of the cravings of their flesh. To do this, you must use the Bible against the people of the church. The Bible is my best friend. You can learn all about the cravings of the flesh in your readings of Galatians 5. Then you must program their minds. It is the secret of control. But this needs to happen willingly, or else you will lose control of your people; then they would turn back to God!"

"Program the mind?" the king said in confusion, "How do I do that?" King Clef asked this question, all along not knowing that his questions were all a part of Satan's plan to control him.

"Well, this is a big secret, you know. And when I was the Chief Musician in Heaven, I kind-of promised God that I would not to tell any humans. God said that humans might use it against one another. So why should I tell an earthly king such a secret? What's in it for me?" asked Satan, with the tactics of a shrewd salesman selling water by a river. His lips curled; his eyes grew red. Satan's hat began to rise off of his head; his horns were growing taller. He was beginning to close the sale.

The king got down on his knees and begged Satan. "Anything, anything! Anything you want, you shall have!" Satan knew that the king's lust for power had overtaken him. Now came the time for Satan to reposition himself into a more controlling role in the kingdom. "Very well, then. Make me your only advisor and heir to the thrown, and you shall have the secret of programming the mind." Satan then snapped his fingers, and a scroll appeared out of a cloud of smoke. "Sign this Declaration of Advisor and Heir." The king agreed, signed the declaration, and placed the royal seal upon the scroll. So it was official. Satan was in position like a coiled snake waiting to strike.

And with a sudden shout, Satan opened his mouth. A piercing sound rang out. The room grew cold like ice. The birds in the cage stopped singing, no chirping, not even a birdcage ringing. The king had become deaf. "I can not hear! Help me, I can not hear!" He screamed in horror.

Satan laughed and said, "You have been deaf to the cries of your own people for years. You have been deaf to the needs of your wife and her tears. You have been deaf to the word of the Lord whom you fear. What more pain is it to lose the sound of a mockingbird; do you know why the cage bird sings?" Then Satan touched the birdcage, and bird fell dead. "That was the sound of death. Did you hear that? Now you are deaf and dumb!" Satan laughed an evil laugh, as the king cried on his knees.

"I suppose I can tell you the secret of programming the minds of the people since you are deaf and all," said Satan.

The king could not hear a thing. He just sat on the floor in sadness. Satan slowly took a bottle from his pocket marked AMOC THE CURE. "Don't worry. Drink this potion and your hearing will return in a day's time. Well, to control masses of people with music, you must use the power of autosuggestion. You do this by---" But in Satan's delusion of grandeur, he heard singing coming from the courtyard. It was three little children holding major sound-fruit and singing the joyous songs that the mothers of the church had taught them:

Jesus loves the little children...

Satan dropped to his knees in pain, as the pure sound of innocent children rang through the air. "This joyous singing in all of its alignment is a curse to my ears! I must run away before they sing the name of Jesus again." Satan silently vanished in a cloud of smoke. The king then rushed to the bottle and drank the cure as fast as he could. He fell on the table in pain, but then quickly he made his way to his bed. A sickness had overtaken him; soon King Clef was not able to move.

When the servants entered the king's chambers, they found the motionless king on his bed with the declaration signed with the king's own pen and crested with the king's royal seal. They picked up the bottle marked "AMOC the Cure" in front of the mirror, and its reflection read: COMA. The servants cried out, "The king has forced a coma upon his body and declared that The Shadow, Luc of Ifer, is now the sole advisor to the king and heir to the Kingdom of Mir!"

CHAPTER 16

AND THERE CAME A time that the people of Mir began to lose more of their children to the Golden Tone of Satan. Satan used his favorite soul-snatcher, the Golden Piper, to take the children in the night. This was a time known as *The Rise of the Golden Piper*. The Golden Piper was a particularly evil demon that did the bidding of Satan by seducing the souls of the young with music. Satan knew that the future of the church rested in the hands of the youth. He also knew that children drew near to exciting new music, because young people are always looking for new ways to express themselves. And since the young did not want to be like their parents, they rebelled by seeking out music they could call their own. Well, you know that Satan was more than happy to accommodate the rebellious youths by sending the Golden Piper.

So beautiful was the music of the evil Golden Piper that the children never thought the piper would cause them any harm. He took the children by song during the dead of night, while their parents were sleeping. As the piper played his music, the children snuck out of their windows, and like mice they followed the music of the piper. And the piper marched all of the children to the evil Golden Tone. If faith cometh by hearing, then the evil Golden Piper cometh in the same manner. The piper came by song, a twisted praise to Satan; the piper was swift like a thief in the night.

The piper played the music of the sweet major sound-fruit while singing the devil's praises in the ears of the children. Once the children were lead to the Golden Tone, the Order of the Golden Tone (the corrupted Royal Ministry) taught the children to feed on the cravings of their flesh with music. But the children did not know that Satan got all of the praise when people fed on the cravings of the flesh (Galatians 5:18).

At that point, I knew that I had to teach the parents of the kingdom all about the principles of Christian music so their children could be saved from the twisted fate of the Golden Tone. So the parents of the Kingdom of Mir joined the Disciples of Christian Music and learned the principles and discernment of music.

CHAPTER 17

THE ORDER OF THE Golden Tone had taken over the Royal ministry. The ministers began to wear graven images of tones around their necks, and they began to sing songs of praise to false idols. "How can I keep the thoughts of the people away from God?" asked one of the Royal Ministers.

Satan became an angry *tone* and struck the minister. "You fool! Your poor mind can not even pay attention! You are a minister in the Order of the Golden Tone. Now focus!" The minister wiped the blood from his bruised lips. Satan continued. "You now wear the graven image of the Golden Tone around your neck. But the Golden Tone that the people worship has hidden within it a small amount of the death sound-fruit. Every time the people mention God, a small sound of death will be released into the air; this will cause them pain. Then the people will sing the songs of the Golden Tone in order to feel pleasure again. They will crave the love of self instead of the love of God."

Then Satan told his Golden Piper to release the sound-fruit of death throughout the kingdom.

The ears of man could not have heard this silent killer of the soul. Only the animals and the dead could have heard it. But dead men tell no tales, and this was *The Rise of the Golden Piper!*

CHAPTER 18

IT WAS NIGHT WHEN Selah returned to the kingdom.

"Something amazing has happened!" Selah shouted with tones of excitement, as he ran into the church. "The Lord has given me an amazing revelation. The Lord has also given unto me a new name. I am no longer Bashiri. My new name is Selah; which means to pause with a musical interlude and meditate on the word of the Lord. He gave me a revelation of music that will change the world!"

At once the disciples stopped what they were doing and came closer to Selah. They were very excited to here this news. Their hearts had been troubled because I was in jail, but Selah came as a ray of hope.

"What is this revelation, Bashiri?" they asked.

Selah closed his eyes in order to see inside of his mind. "I have been given a great revelation of music. I have seen a vision of the musical gateways of Heaven and Hell. Listen closely, as I teach you this vision." And at once, the disciples moved closer.

Selah continued, "God gave me these revelations

and warnings as I have written them on this scroll:

God's Law of Sound and the Star of David
(major and minor, overtones vs. undertones,
and the Divine shapes of sound)

We speak in song (Eph. 5:19)

The Song of Moses (Programming the Mind)

Three Admonitions
The Warning of Psalm 1:1-6
The Warning of St. Jude 1:10
The Warning of Jesus- Mark 4:24

"But before we begin, let us pray". After the prayer, Selah continued. "Let us begin by remembering the three main principles of Christian music:

Be Ye Led By The Spirit
Be Ye Rooted In Christ
Be Ye Wise In Musical Knowledge

"The Lord showed me the words of Jesus: '*For nothing is hidden, except to be revealed; nor has anything been secret, but that it would come to light*' (Mark 4:22, NASB). The Lord also spoke to my heart saying '*My people are destroyed for lack of knowledge*' (Hosea 4:6).

"If you are ready for the truth, then stay and hear this revelation. If you are fearful, then leave while your ears are shielded from responsibility and your mind is protected by a childlike innocence!"

And Selah shared the depth of the revelations and warnings. The minds of the people were becoming wise in musical knowledge. The people were opening the Great Gift of Music.

CHAPTER 19

AND THERE CAME A time when the king's faithful servant took Selah to the castle in secrecy. The servant knew of the story from the book of First Samuel that spoke of a time that King Saul had been cursed by evil spirits. The Bible tells us that King Saul sent for a skilled musician to play music that would drive out the evil spirits. In ancient times, it was widely known that music could break the curse of evil. So the servants of the king found a young musician named David. The young David brought his skillful music to play for the king. And the Bible tells us that the music of David caused the evil spirits to depart from King Saul, and the king was made well.

So when Selah entered the king's private chambers, he brought with him the Bible and three sound-fruit (two major sound-fruit and the sound of faith). He held the three-fold sound-fruit in the air and sang the words of Psalm 23. And with a burst of light, the sound-fruit joined together like morning stars (Job 38:7). A warm glow filled the air, and a rainbow of sound was seen from its beginning to the end. The ears of the king began to flare like nostrils as the aroma of sweet music filled his heart. The breath of life filled his dead soul, and the king rose from his bed like Lazarus rose from the tomb (John 11:43). The curse of the coma had been lifted from the king.

"Oh, thank you for restoring my health and my hearing! Now I will take my thrown back, and the people shall stop chasing religion and God," the king shouted in anger.

"But by God you are healed. Does not your heart belong to God in the name of Jesus?" asked Selah.

King Clef turned his head away like a whip and arrogantly proclaimed, "There is no God!"

The king's servant held his head down in shame like a beaten dog. The words of the king had broken his spirit. But it was at this time that a child-servant walked into the room. Upon hearing the words of the king, the child said, "King, why do you not believe in God? Are you simple or something?"

"How dare you talk to me like that! I am the King, not a simpleton. There is no such thing as God!" shouted the king in red fury.

"Well, do you know everything in the world?" the child innocently asked.

" No, nobody does," the king replied.

"Well, do you know at least half of everything?" the child asked.

The king was growing more annoyed by the child's

questions, but still he replied, "Yes, you worthless child-servant. I do know half of everything in the world. Now why do you ask these stupid questions?"

The child replied, "Well, do you not think that God might be in the other half of stuff that you do not know?"

The king fell speechless. "Matthew 21:16, *Out of the mouths of babes...*" he thought.

Selah was very impressed by the child. "You should listen to the young one; for she speaks the truth. King Clef, the spell has been broken, and you have your life back. But be not confused; you have witnessed the power of the Almighty God! God placed much power in the sound-fruit. All of this time you have been feasting on the lust for power. A lust that Satan had been serving you. But you can be forgiven today. All you have to do is pray the sinner's pray with me and invite the Lord, Jesus Christ, into your heart. You can change your lust for power into a thirst for Christ. You can change your love for money into a love for God."

And Selah reached out his hand to the king. The king took the right hand of fellowship. And on bended knee, the King of Mir prayed to the King of Kings and Lord of Lords, The God of Abraham and the God of Moses. King Clef was moved be the words of Selah. On his knees, he prayed and invited Jesus into his heart. His Christian walk had begun. The Disciples of Christian Music are truly in the soul-saving business.

And then the king told his servant to release Otto from the jail. The time had come for the king to join Selah and Otto; they had to release the people from the Order of the Golden Tone.

CHAPTER 20

OTTO AND SELAH FORCED their way through the worshipping crowd to reach the steps of the altar of the Golden Tone. Bashiri, the student, was now Selah, the teacher. Otto proudly watched the annointed teacher address the crowd of pagan worshippers.

Selah spoke to the crowd saying, "People of the Kingdom of Mir, is your music dead? It must be dead! If it were alive, it would seek to serve and glorify its creator. Since your music does not glorify God, the true Creator, then your music is dead to God!

"It was God who created music in the Garden of Good and Evil, and the fruits of sound know their creator. Your music must be dead! Because if it were alive, your music would shout the name of the Lord, even when your words do not. God gave music to man so that man would glorify Him with it. Music cannot live without living its purpose. Jesus says that you shall know a tree by its fruit, and so shall you know your music is alive when it glorifies God, Jehovah!

"When your music comes alive, it is not longer a thing of man; it is a new creature. When your music comes alive in Christ for its true purpose of glorifying God, it will take on a new name like Abram became Abraham, Jacob became Israel, and Saul became Paul. Your music shall from that point forth be called *Praise*, and it will live as Praise without compromise all the days of its life! My people, God does not want your music, God wants your praise.

"Satan was once the anointed cherub, but now he is the fallen tone. The touch of Satan is the death of music. But now I call you, Satan, out of music in the name of Jesus!"

And in the name of Jesus, the demons of Satan began to leave the music of the people. You could see the evil clouds of smoke scatter in the wind. And at once the music of the Golden Tone had stopped, and the worshippers were released from Satan's music.

"Now music shall be known by its new name in Jesus. The Music of God shall be called PRAISE!" Selah held the Fruit of the Spirit high in the air and the sea of wind parted. Then a great light flowed like a rainbow from all of the sound-fruit in the kingdom. The lights then joined with the Fruit of the Spirit and filled the sky with a burst of glorious sound! The music of the people had become Praise; for this was the birth of the new Music Ministry. And the people let out a mighty shout of praised to God, Jehovah. "Now, Praise, arise out of your tomb of fleshly music! Arise and live in your true purpose: TO GLORIFY GOD

AND TO EDIFY MAN! Arise, ye Praise! Arise in the name of Jesus!" Then the sound-fruit went into the soul of the people. And when the fruit united with the souls, a immaculate conception took place. The souls of the righteous had birthed praise out of their hearts, but the souls of the ungodly had birthed secular music out of their bellies.

And God saw that music was now birthed from the people; then God sent an angel to close the gates of the Garden of Good and Evil. And God spoke to the world in the great voice of a mighty rushing wind, "Music has now been placed into the hearts of everyone in the world. From this day forth, I shall only hear Praise birthed out of the righteous. Music of the ungodly; depart from Me; for I do not know you. The deception of your music is the conception of your wickedness. The conception of your music is wicked from its unholy union. Your music had lain down with witches and warlocks, and harlots and demons.

"You all must follow My Laws of Sound. My children, I do not seek your music; I desire your praise. Where there is Praise, so shall I be. For I am the great I AM!"

And now you know the secrets of music. My mission is done, but your mission is just beginning...

EPILOGUE

IT IS SO IMPORTANT that you read both 'Music in the Garden of Good and Evil' and 'Music and the Star of David'. Book One is the Story of Music, and Book Two is the Secret of Music. The knowledge in these books are what every minister of music (choir directors, musicians, and singers), pastor, and parent should know in this ever changing world of influence. Tell others about these books. Each one reach one.

Did you know that with all of the musical knowledge of Satan, that wicked snake cannot even make music on this earth? Man was given dominion over the things of this earth. Have you ever noticed that all good and evil music on earth has come from men and women? The devil did not even have to create evil music. I know this because the Bible tells us that "the imagination of man's heart is evil from his youth" (Genesis 8:13).

The great deceiver seeks to tempt our imaginations in order to draw out evil music. The evil in music is from man. The devil has been getting too much credit for shining a lamp into dirty minds and saying he brought the dirt. All Satan did was use smoke and mirrors in order to keep you distracted; then evil thoughts were able to run unchecked through the house of your mind destroying what it will. How can your music be a light unto the world without first shining the light onto itself?

My friends, these principles will break Satan's hold on our music. Turn your music into Praise; do not turn your praise into music. The music of man is dead to God. But when music is born again as Praise, God will receive it. So do as the last words in the Book of Psalms say and 'Praise ye the Lord' (Psalm 150).

ABOUT THE AUTHOR

Lorne Lee is the author of the ground-breaking books *'Music in the Garden of Good and Evil'* and *'Music and the Star of David'*. He has a long history as a music professor, band director, Minister of Music, clinician, consultant, composer, arranger, and adjudicator.

Lorne has held the positions of Director of Bands and Instructor of Music at Johnson C. Smith University in Charlotte, NC, Associate Director of Bands at Livingstone College in Salisbury, NC, and Director of Bands and Assistant Professor of Music at Savannah State University in Savannah, GA.

Lorne Lee has Bachelor of Music from The University of Central Oklahoma in Edmond, OK and a Master of Music from Howard University in Washington, D.C.

www.ingramcontent.com/pod-product-compliance
Lightning Source LLC
Chambersburg PA
CBHW021450240626
47154CB00005B/1787